ZOOM AWAY

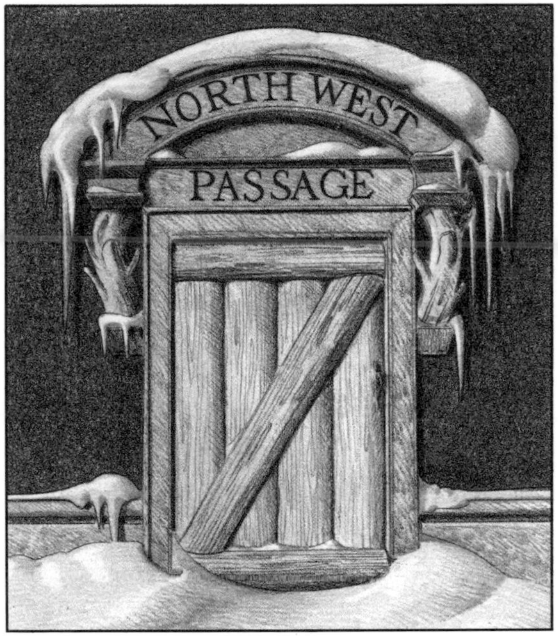
NORTH WEST
PASSAGE

BY Tim Wynne-Jones PICTURES BY Ken Nutt

A Groundwood Book
Douglas & McIntyre
Toronto • Vancouver

Zoom was knitting something warm. Outside, it was summer. All the other cats were in their light summer coats, chasing butterflies, rolling in the grass. But Zoom was going on an adventure.

When he had packed his supplies, Zoom took a cab to his friend Maria's house. He knocked three times on her big front door.

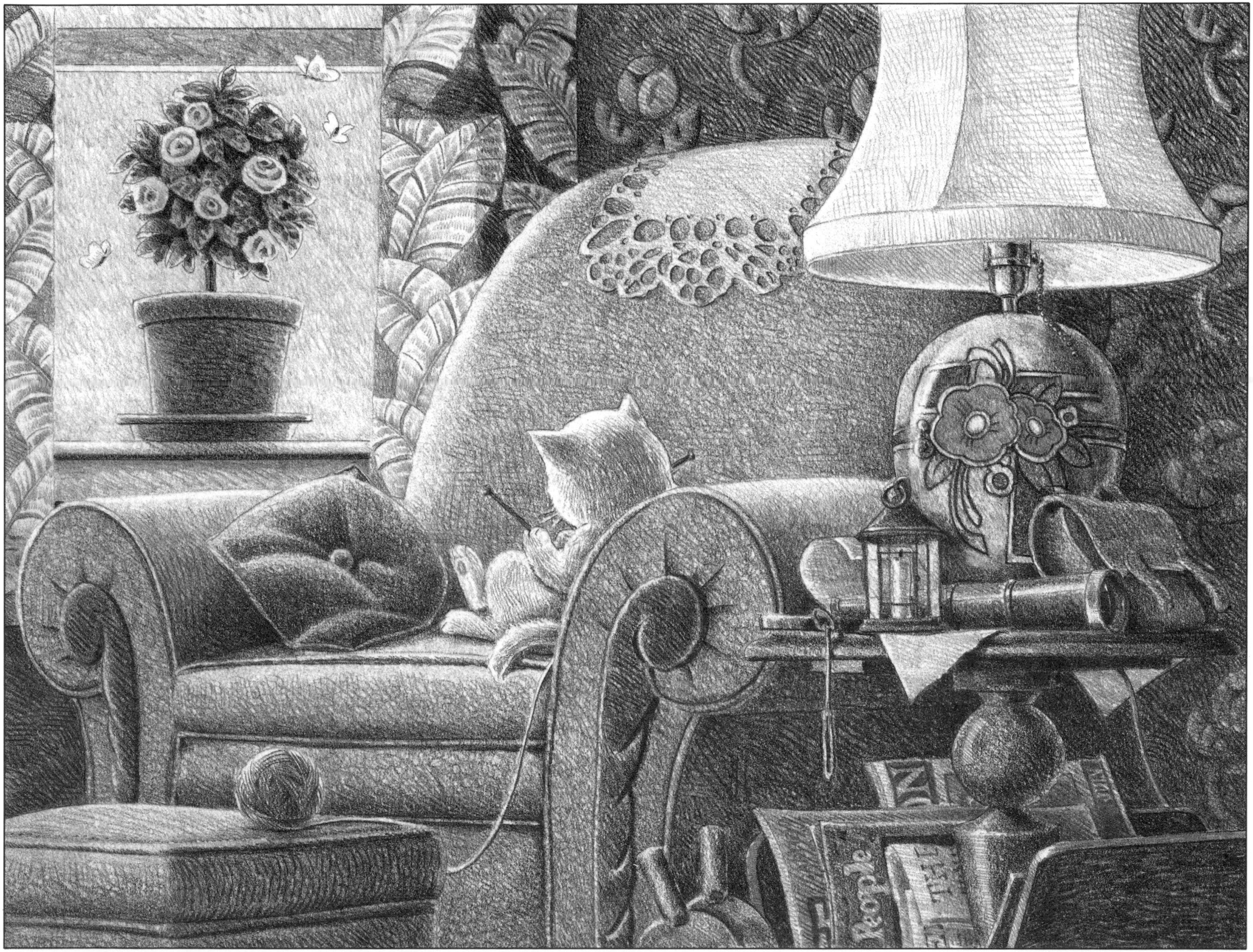
People

Maria was dressed in the fluffiest coat Zoom had ever seen.

"There's no time to lose," she said, and showed Zoom a map of the North Pole.

"I received a letter from your uncle, Captain Roy, some months ago," she said. "He was going to sail to the North Pole. He hasn't written since. Will you come with me and search for him in the High Arctic?"

"Yes," said Zoom.

"Good," said Maria.

Zoom put on his back pack and they started up the wide staircase in the front hall.

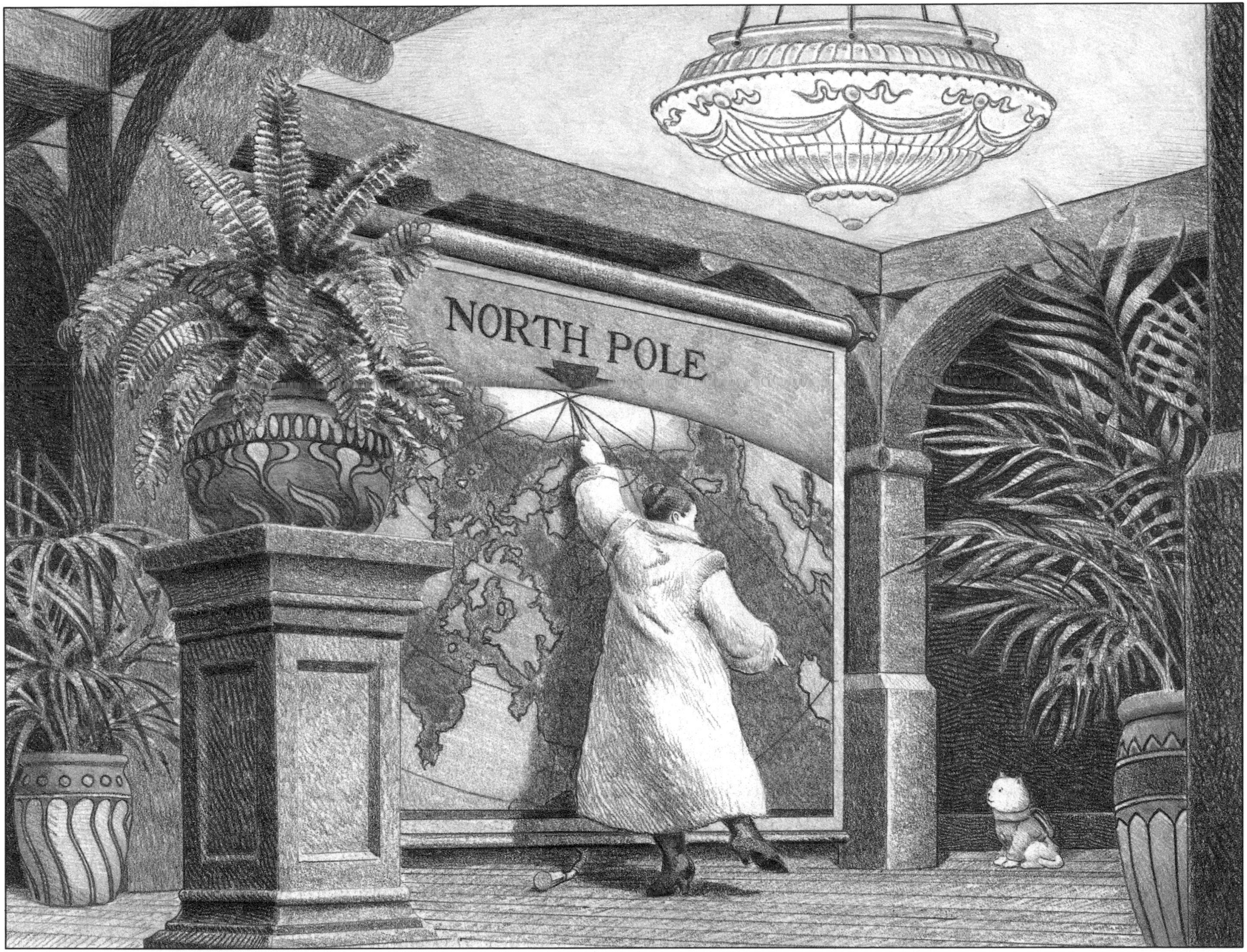
NORTH POLE

Zoom had never been upstairs at Maria's before. The way was very steep. The air grew cold. There were little hills of snow in the corners of each step. The windows on the landing were prickly with ice, and long icicles hung like teeth from the archway. The hall was carpeted with snow. Zoom put on his ping-pong paddle snow shoes.

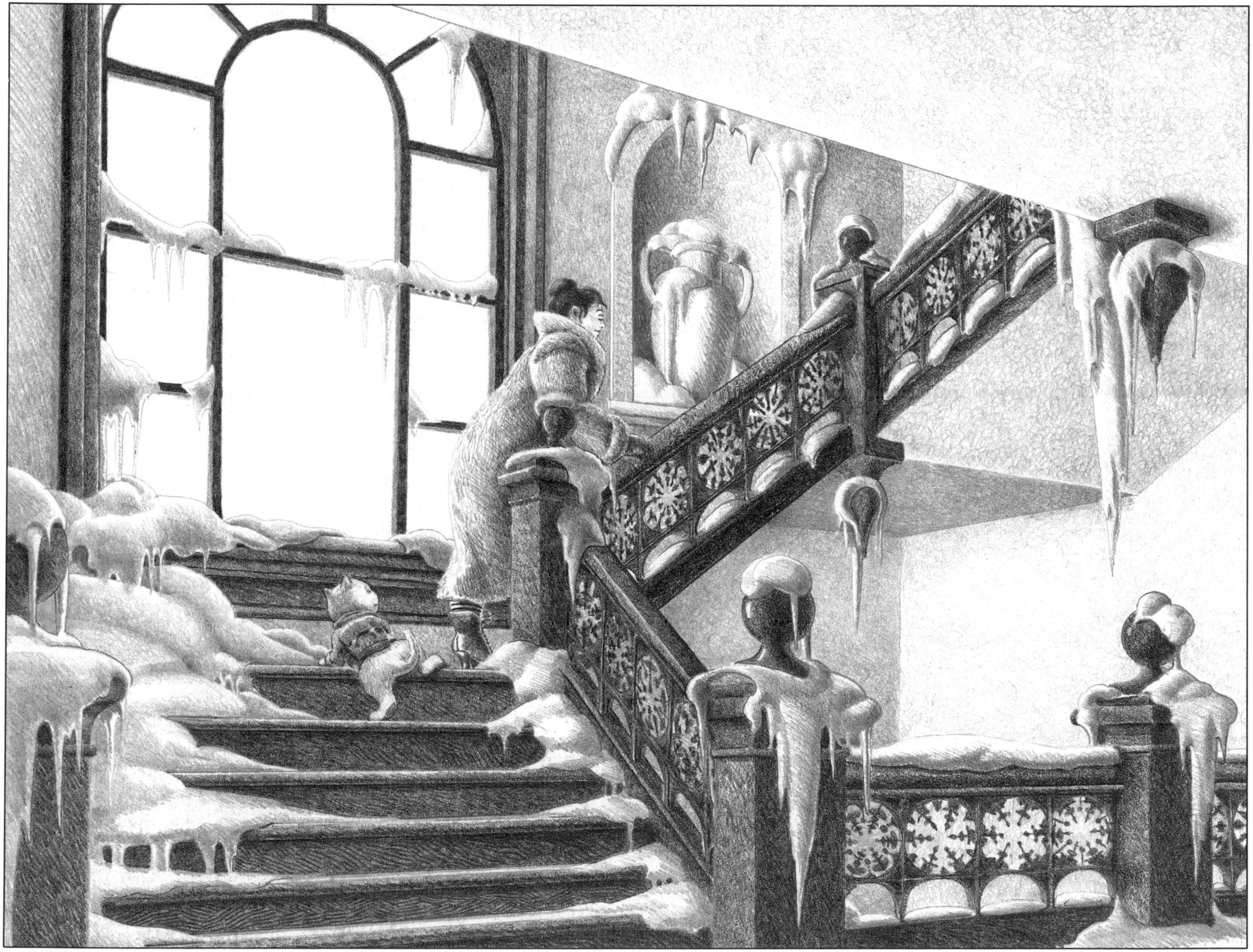

From a dark room Zoom heard the howling of wolves.

"Owwwwwwww."

Maria suggested they sing a song so as not to be afraid.

Zoom followed Maria down corridor after corridor, from room to room. There was deep snow everywhere now.

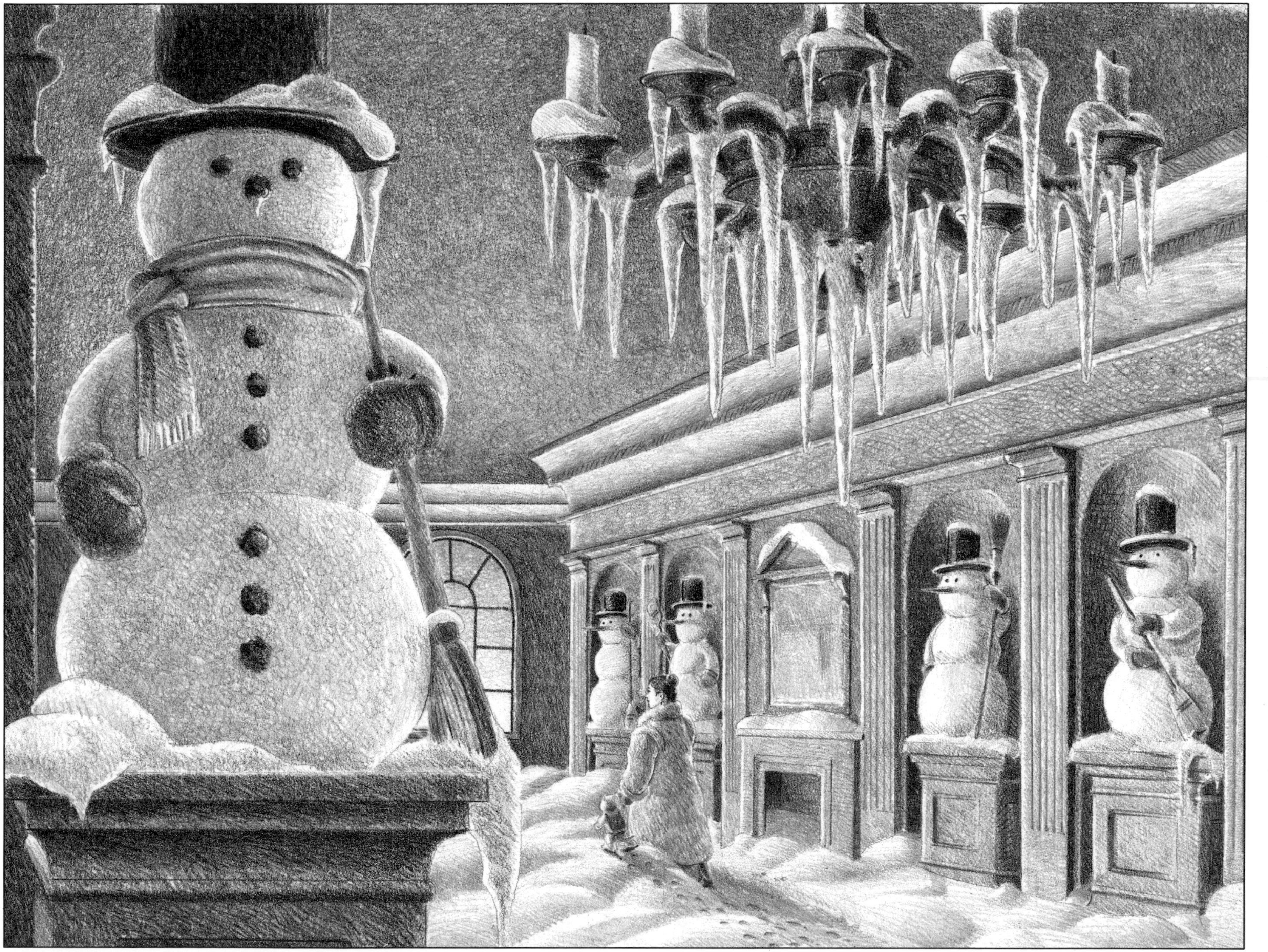

At last Maria stopped and checked her astrolabe.

"This will be a good place for lunch," she said.

They brushed the snow off two comfy chairs. Zoom placed tin cups on a frozen end table and Maria filled each one with tomato soup from a thermos bottle.

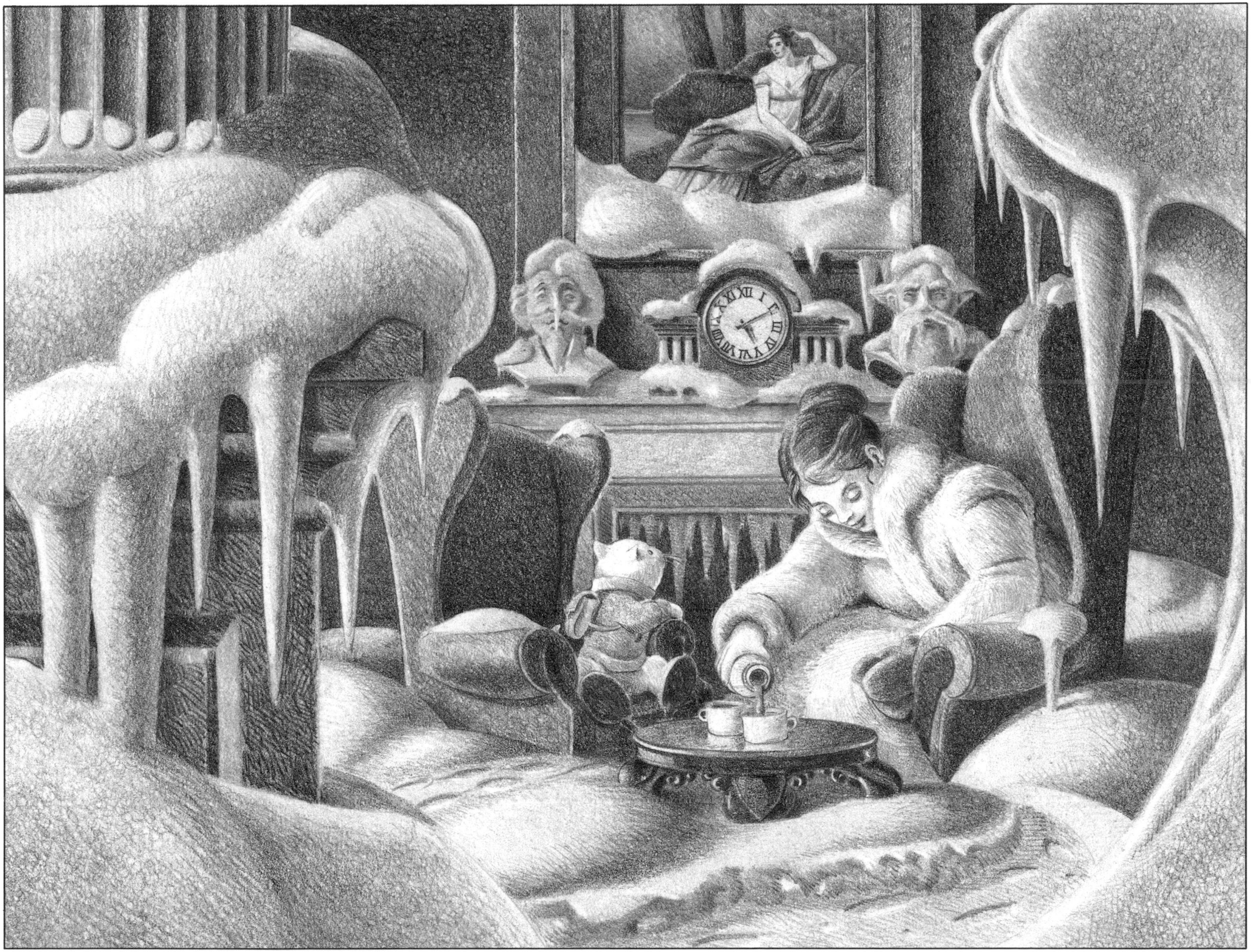

Not long after lunch they came to a narrow hall which led to a little room. There was a low door in the wall with the words "Northwest Passage" carved in wood over it. Zoom could hear the wind whistling and thumping against the other side.

He put on his goggles. Maria opened the door.

Oh, how the wind howled — louder and more ferocious than a pack of wolves.

Zoom lit his lantern. The doorway was very small. Too small for Maria.

"I'll have to find a different way," she said. "I'll meet you on the other side."

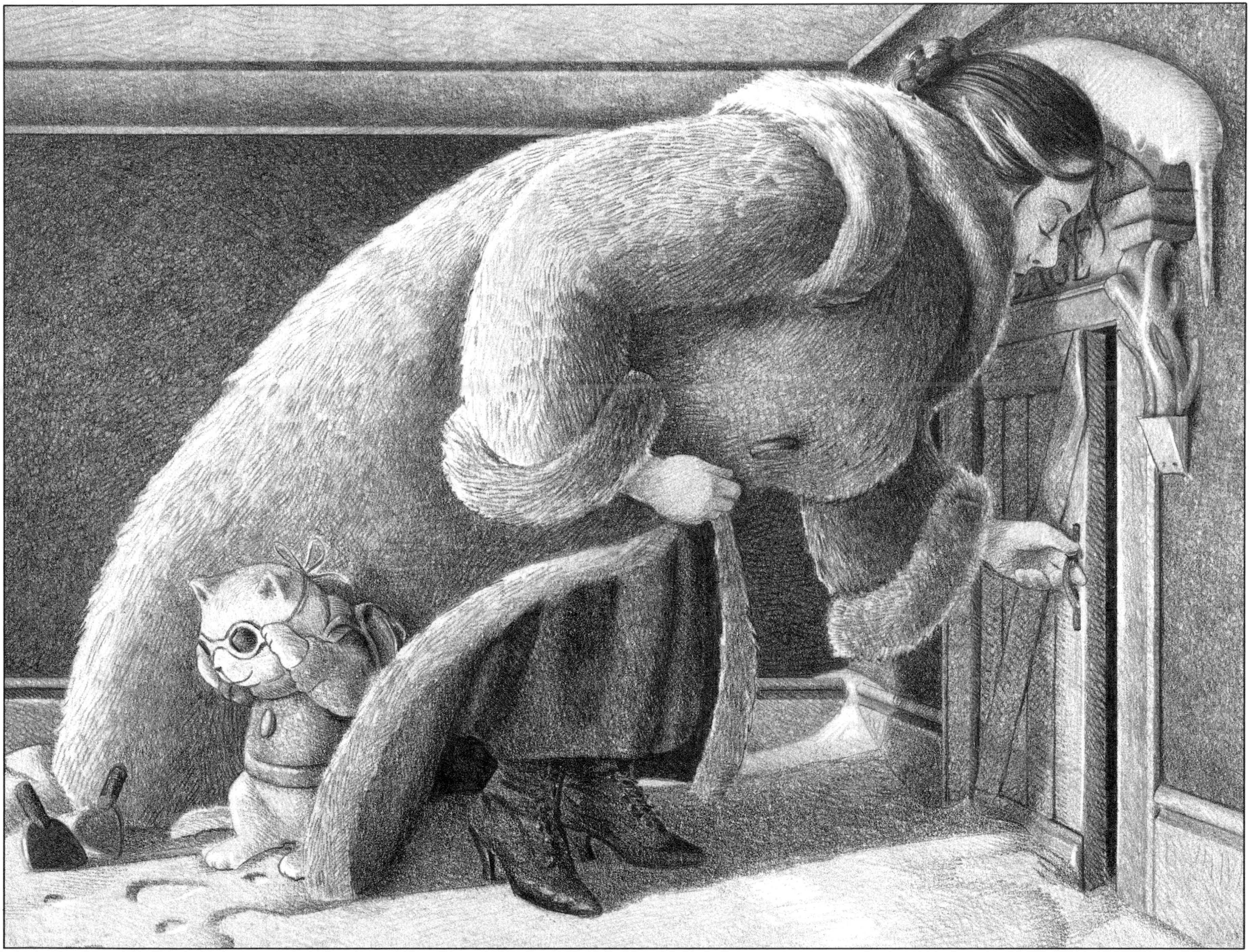

Zoom set off. It was very dark and very cold. Soon his paws were numb. Frost tugged at his whiskers.

I hope it isn't much farther, he thought.

Then he saw the light up ahead — the end of the tunnel.

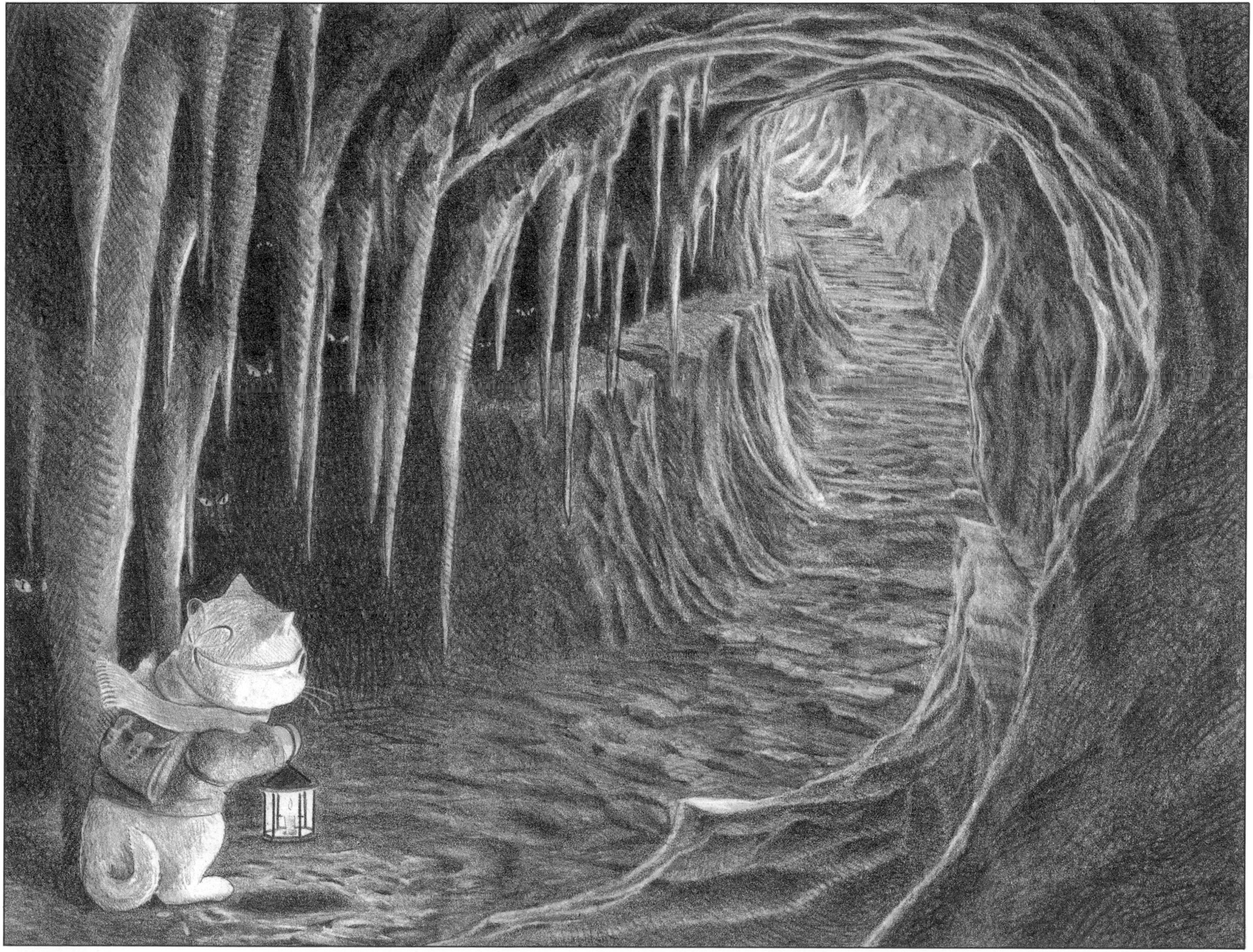

Zoom scampered out into the light.
Everywhere was ice, glistening and glaring in the
bright sun. The air smelled like the sea.
"Yahoo!" he cried. "The North Pole."

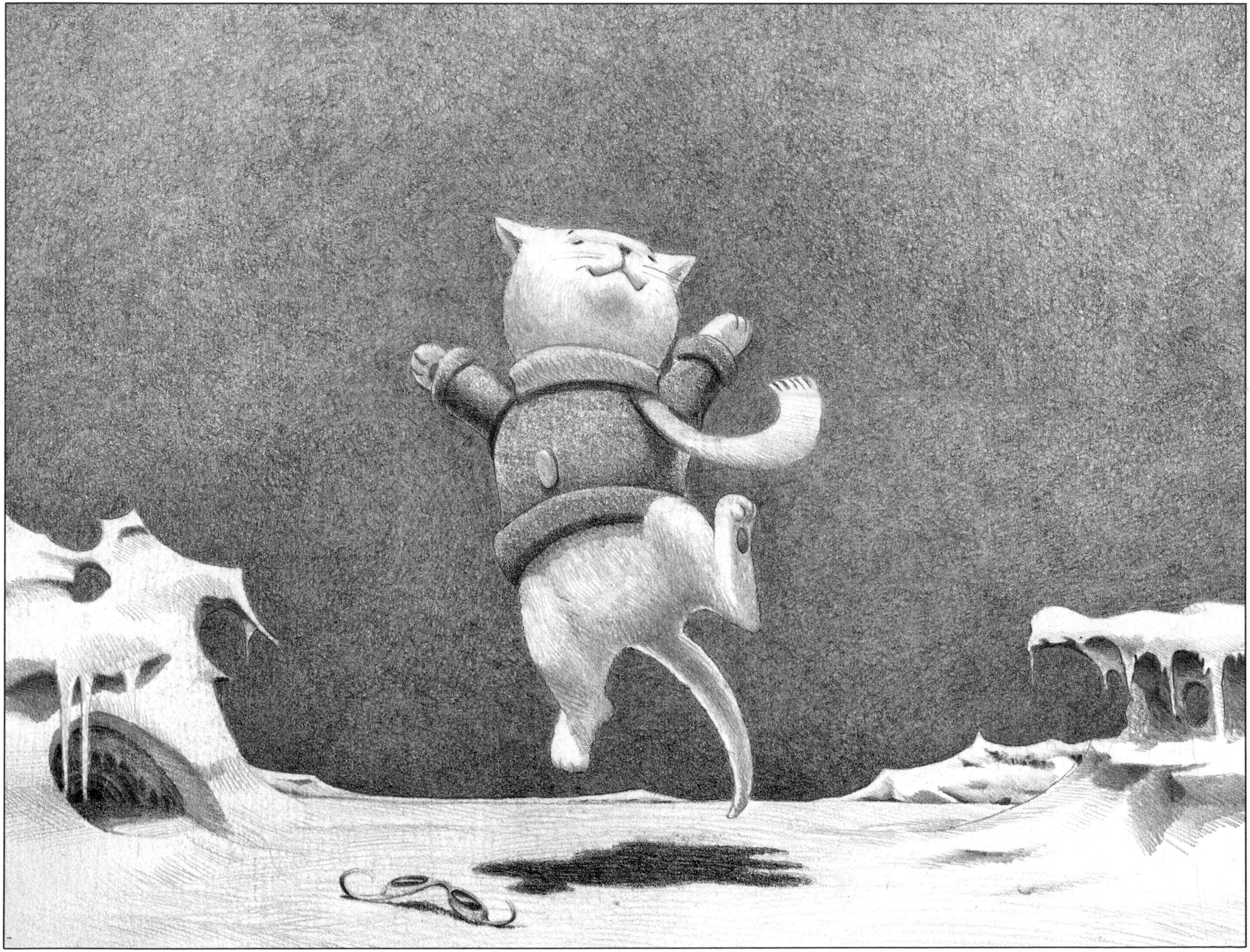

Zoom tied on his skates.

"Whee!" he shouted. "I'm skating on the Arctic Sea."

Round and round the wind twirled him. Birds circled laughing. Seals barked and clapped. Zoom didn't feel cold any more.

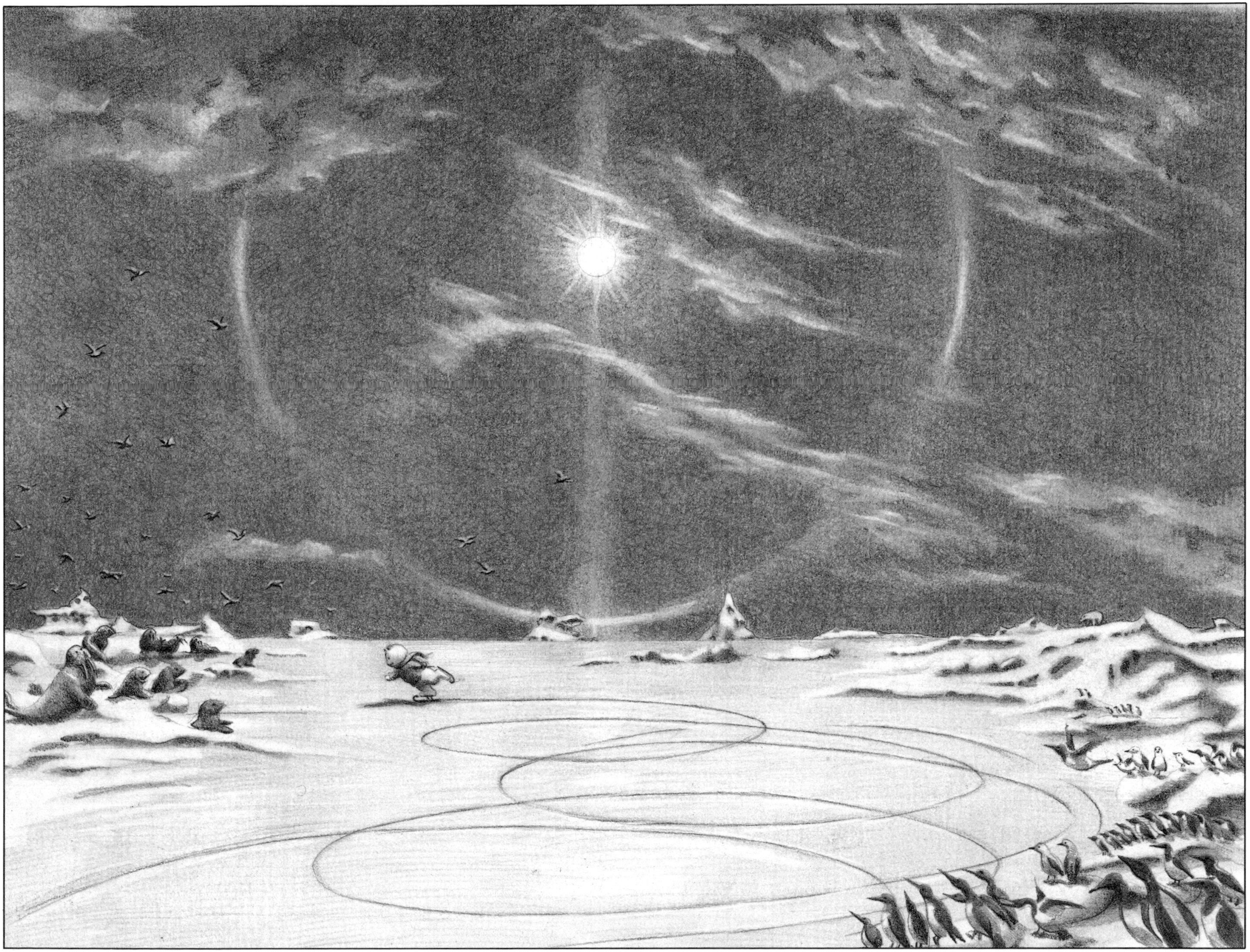

But after a while he got very tired. Out of breath, he clambered to the top of a frozen hill. He took out his spy glass to look around.

There was a ship stuck in the ice.

"The Catship," he read on the bow. It was Uncle Roy's boat.

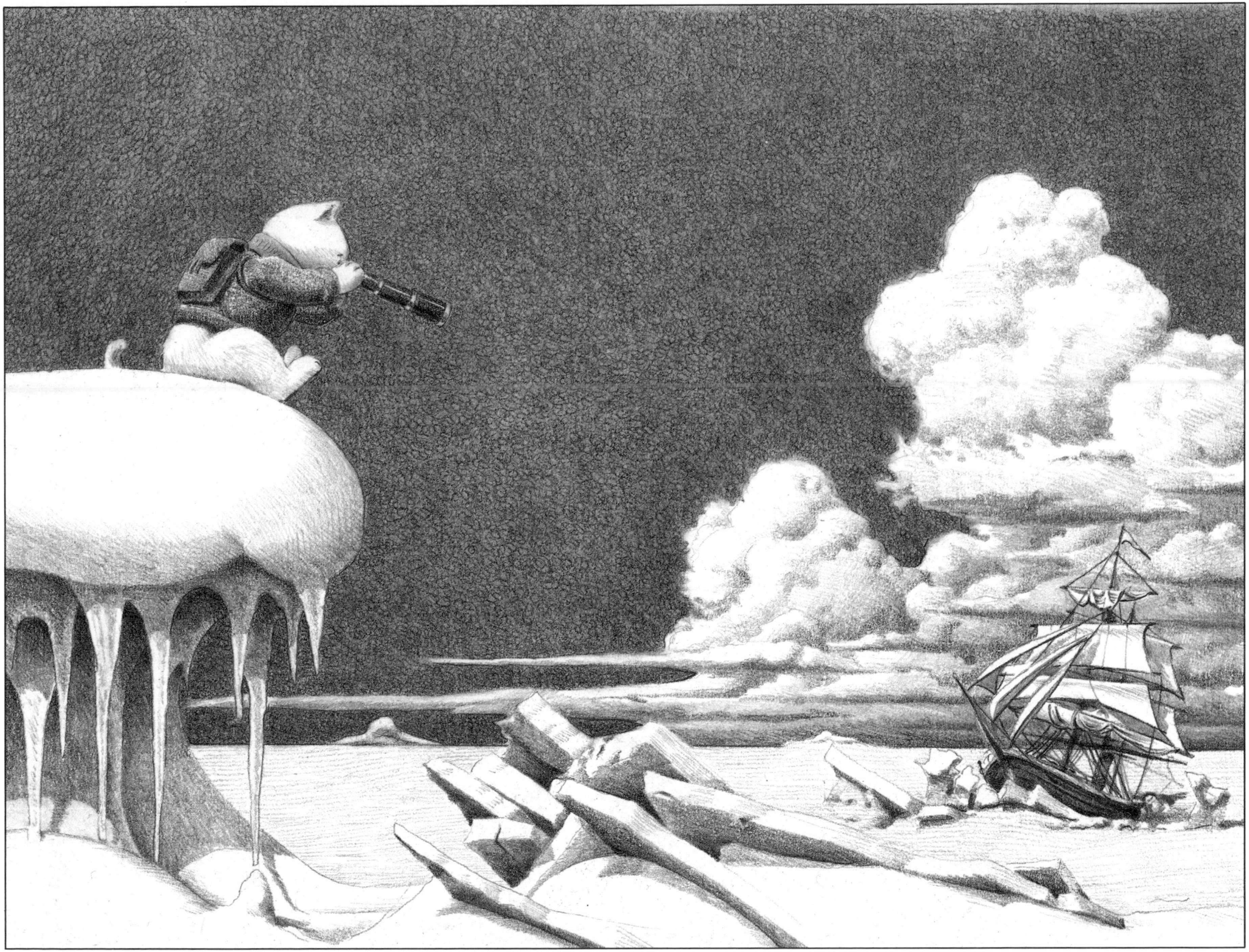

It didn't take long to get there.

The ship was on an angle. It looked very lonely.

"Hello," called Zoom. There didn't seem to be anyone on board.

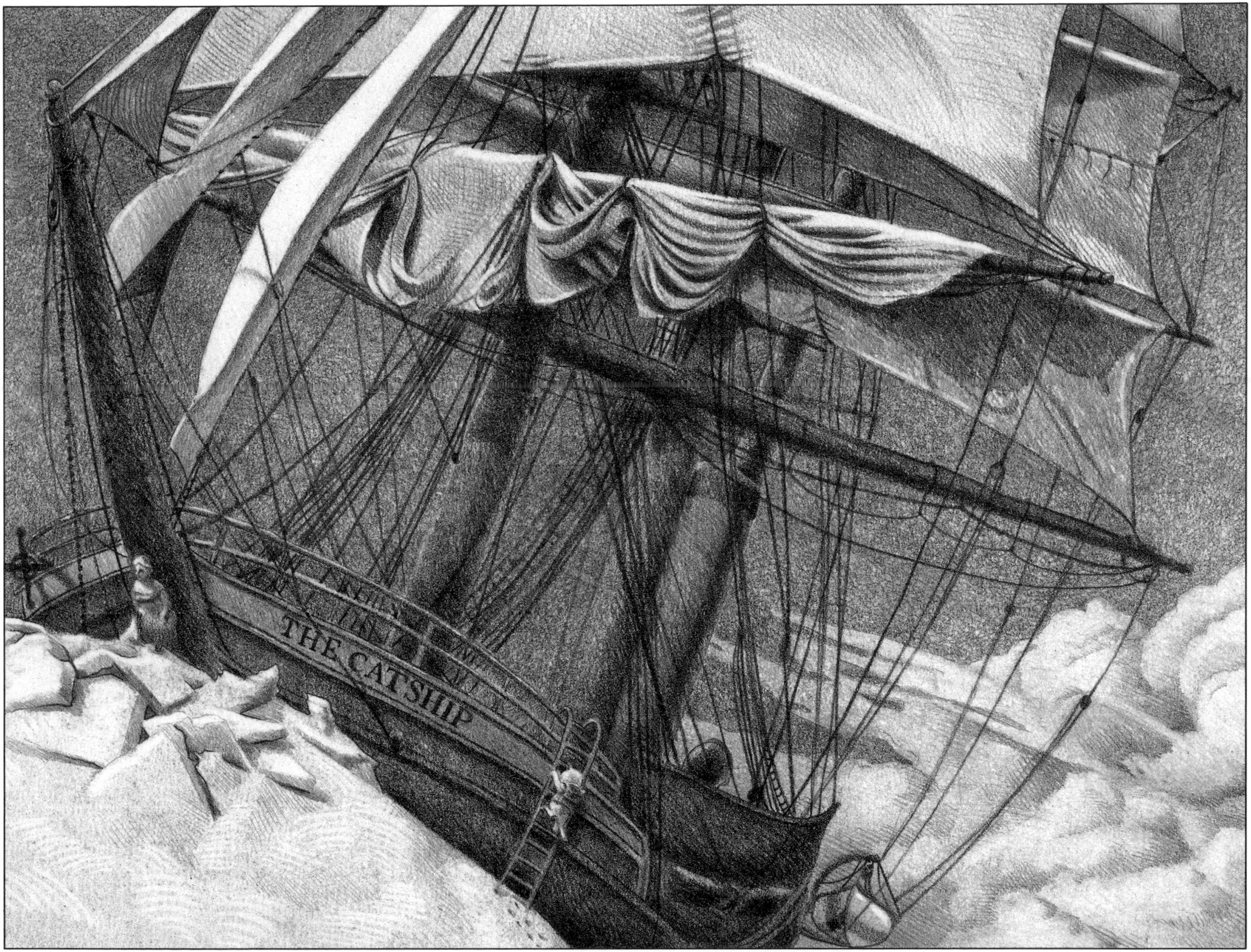
THE CATSHIP

In the galley there was a note on the table.

To whom it may concern:
My crew and I have boarded a passing
iceberg and are heading south. We have
lots of food and water and are in a merry
mood. Be sure to give my love to Maria
and my trusty nephew Zoom if you
should meet them in your travels.

Yours affectionately,
Captain Roy.

P.S. I'll be back for the Catship when the
ice melts.

Beside the note was a captain's whistle.

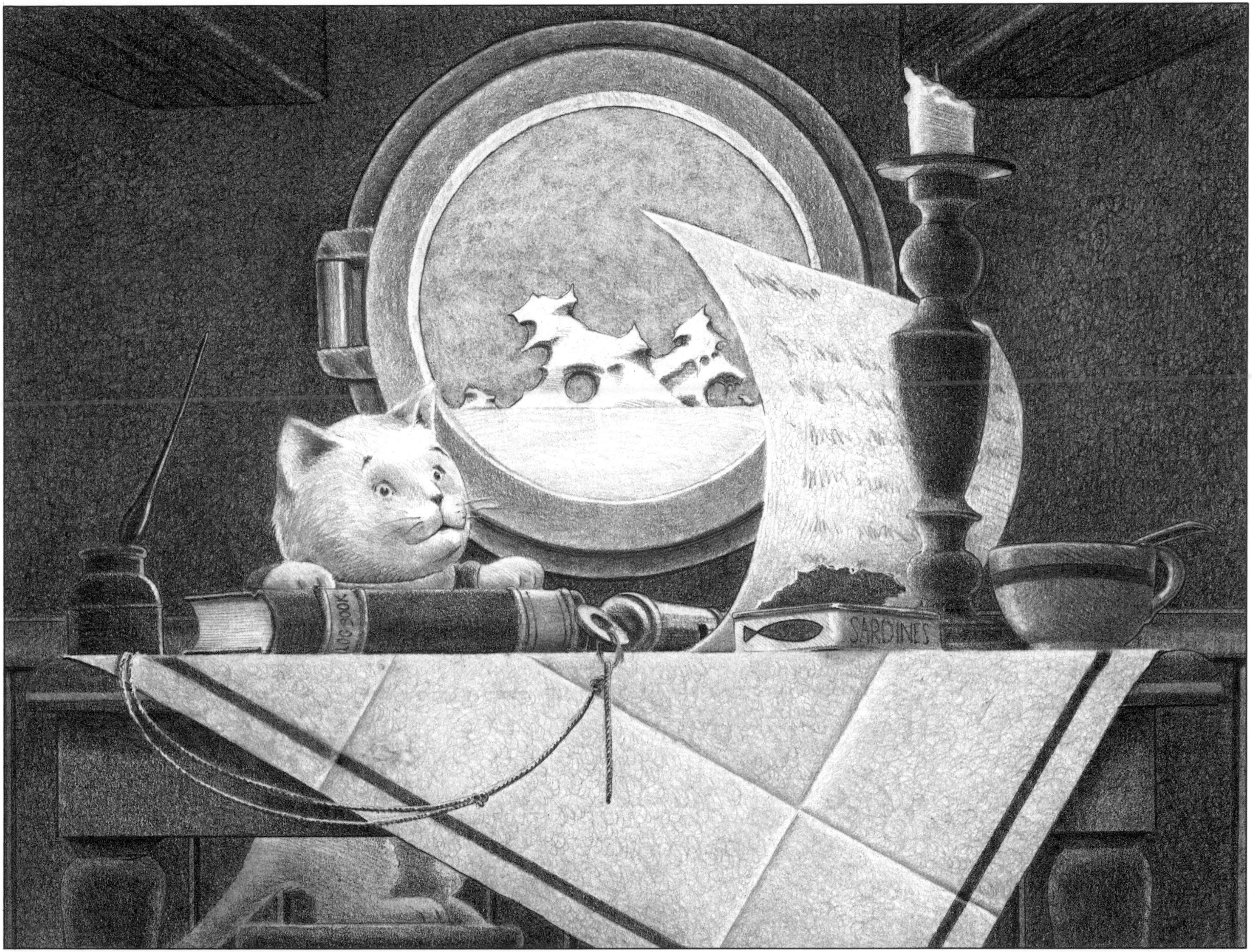
SARDINES

Zoom put the whistle around his neck. He looked through a porthole out at the snow. He felt sad. He had hoped to see his uncle.

"Zoooooom!" Somebody was calling his name.

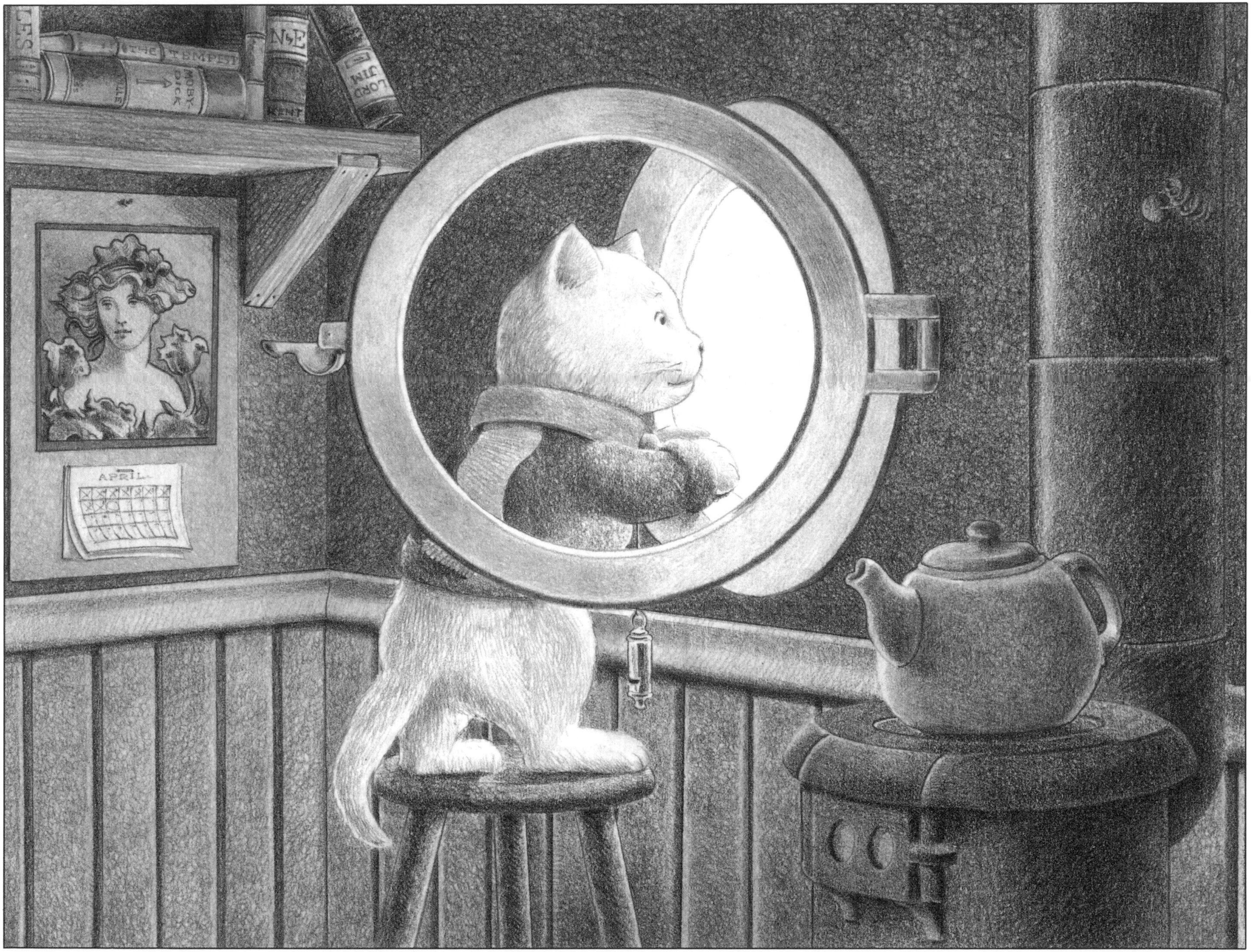
MOBY-DICK
LORD JIM
KENT
APRIL

It was Maria. She had made a sled out of two oars and some sailcloth.

"I'm glad to see you," said Zoom and climbed onto the sled. Then he told her about the note and the iceberg and Uncle Roy's escape.

He yawned. Maria tucked Zoom in nice and cozy.

"It's all down hill from here," she said.

Zoom drifted happily off to sleep with the arctic sun beaming down on his face.

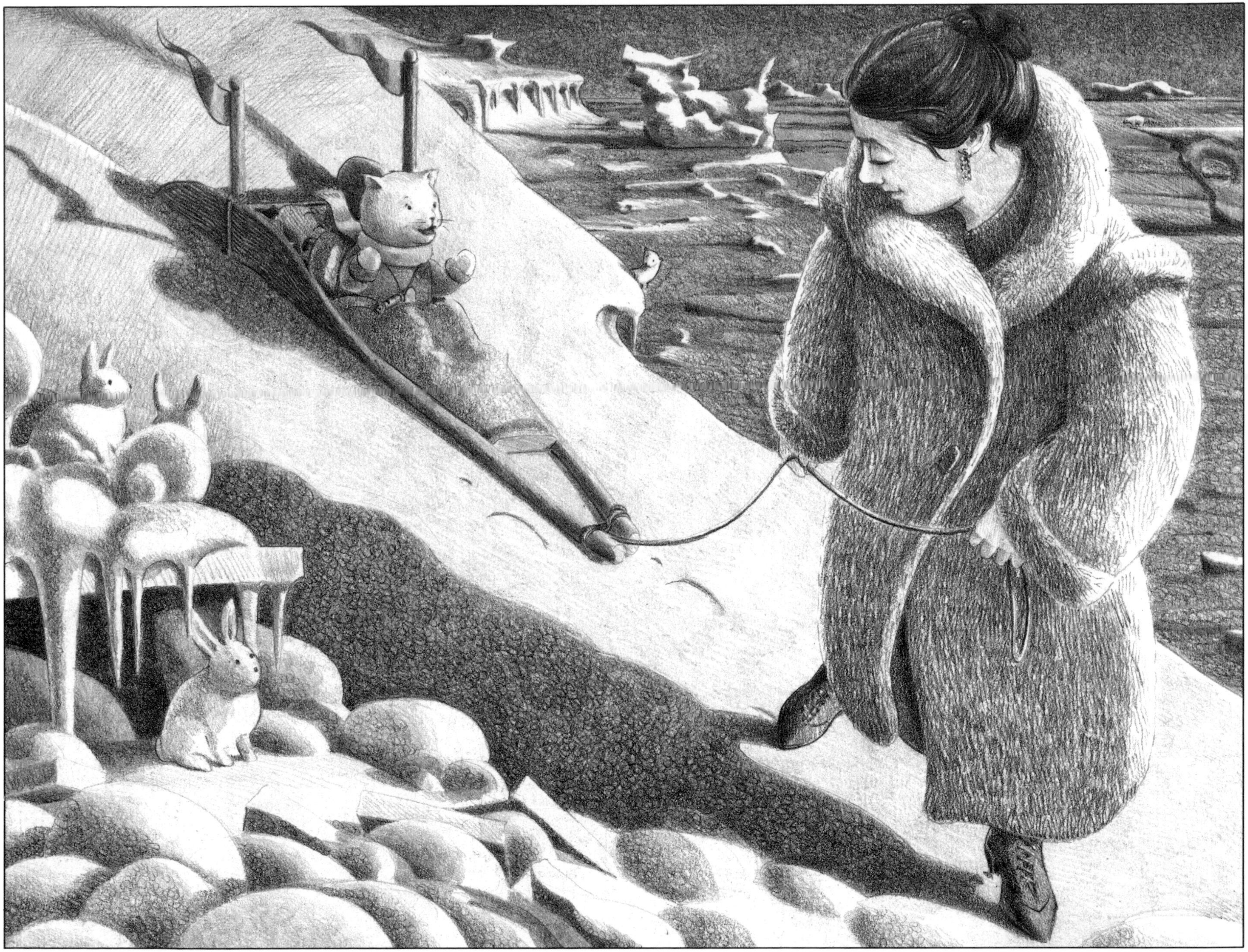

When Zoom woke up he was curled in the wing-chair in front of the fireplace in Maria's sitting room. Maria was asleep on the chaise longue.

Zoom licked his paws and snuggled down again. He had been having a nice dream about travelling with Maria and Uncle Roy to rescue the Catship once the ice melted.

He closed his eyes.

He hoped it wouldn't be too long.

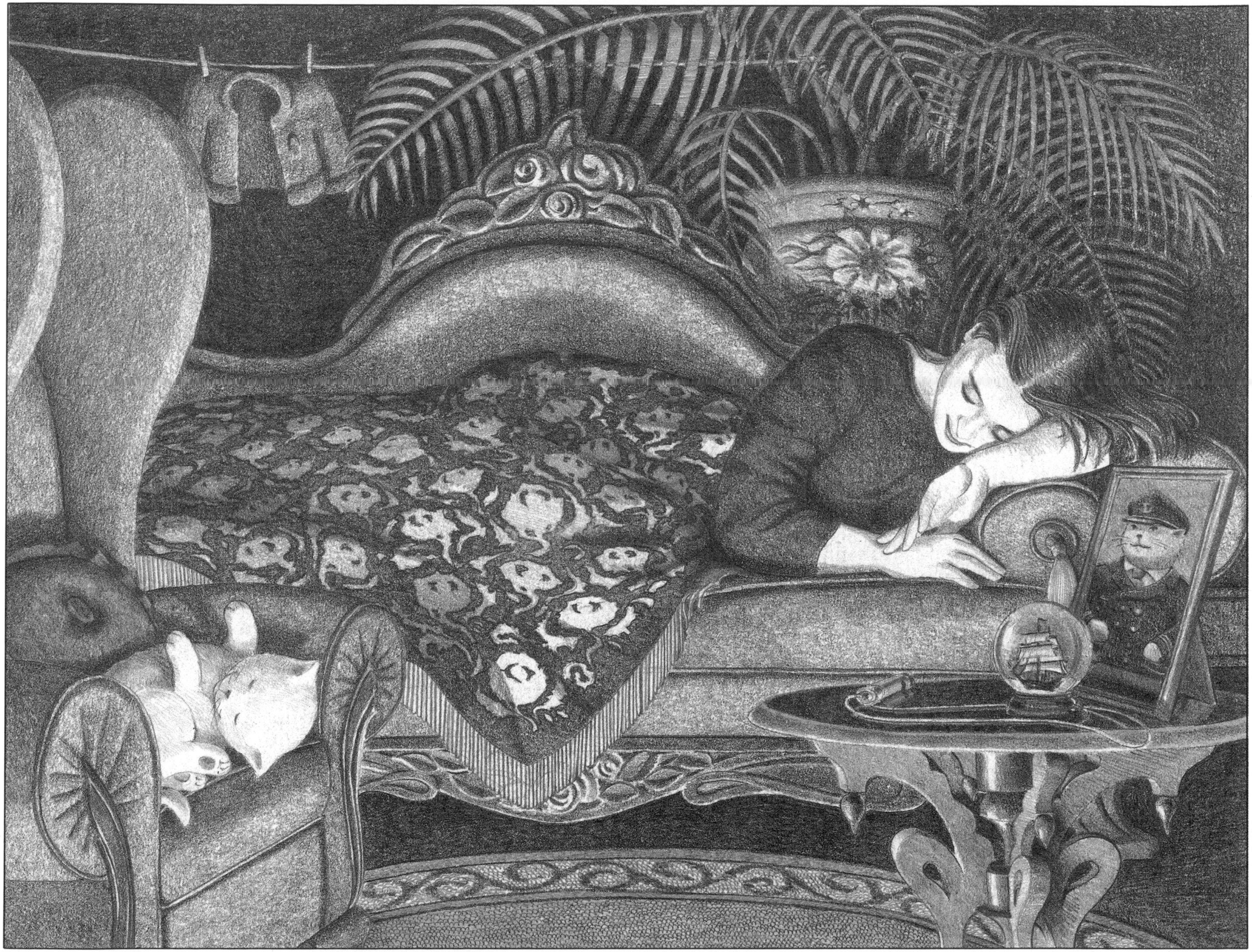

For Xan and Maddy
TWJ

Text copyright © 1985 by Tim Wynne-Jones
Illustrations copyright © 1985 Ken Nutt

Second printing 1986

A Groundwood Book
Douglas & McIntyre Ltd.
1615 Venables Street
Vancouver, British Columbia

Canadian Cataloguing in Publication Data
Wynne-Jones, Tim.
 Zoom Away

ISBN 0-88899-042-1

I. Nutt, Ken. 1951- II. Title

PS8595.Y59Z39 1985   jc813′.54   C85-098902-7
PZ7.W96Zoo 1985

Design by Michael Solomon

Printed and bound in Hong Kong
by Everbest Printing Co., Ltd.